GREEN LANTERN

IS RESPONSIBLE

Written By
CHRISTOPHER HARBO

Illustrated by
OTIS FRAMPTON

Capstone Young Readers
a capstone imprint

Green Lantern is responsible. He thinks before he acts and always does his job. People can depend on him to do his best.

When Green Lantern takes an oath, he follows it for life.

Green Lantern is responsible because he always keeps his promises.

IN BRIGHTEST DAY, IN BLACKEST NIGHT
NO EVIL SHALL ESCAPE MY SIGHT
LET THOSE WHO WORSHIP EVIL'S MIGHT
BEWARE MY POWER
GREEN LANTERN'S LIGHT!

When people are in danger, Green Lantern always lends a hand.

The Galactic Guardian is responsible because he helps people in need.

When Green Lantern says he'll help someone,
he always follows through.

Green Lantern is responsible because he stays true to his word.

When Green Lantern fights for justice, he gives it all he's got.

The Galactic Guardian is responsible because he always does his best.

When Green Lantern stops crime, he makes sure that no one gets hurt.

Green Lantern is responsible because he sets
a good example.

When Green Lantern solves a problem, he plans his moves carefully.

Green Lantern is responsible because he thinks about the results of his actions.

When Green Lantern stumbles, he gets up and tries again.

The Galactic Guardian is responsible because he never, ever gives up.

When Green Lantern makes a mess, he doesn't walk away from it.

Green Lantern is responsible because he helps clean up.

Green Lantern acts responsibly whenever super-villains strike.

And he holds them responsible for their actions too!

GREEN LANTERN SAYS...

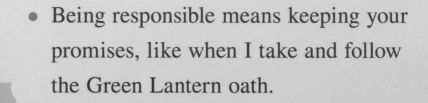

- Being responsible means keeping your promises, like when I take and follow the Green Lantern oath.

- Being responsible means helping people in need, like when I rescue a family in danger.

- Being responsible means setting a good example, like when I use my power ring to protect people from harm.

- Being responsible means cleaning up after yourself, like when I tidy up after battling Vandal Savage.

- Being responsible means being the best you that you can be!

BE YOUR BEST
with the World's Greatest Super Heroes!

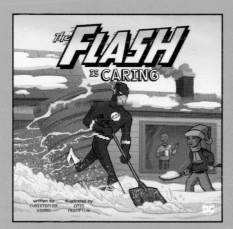

ONLY FROM CAPSTONE!

DC Super Heroes Character Education
is published by Capstone Young Readers
A Capstone Imprint
1710 Roe Crest Drive
North Mankato, Minnesota 56003
www.mycapstone.com

Editor: Julie Gassman
Designer: Hilary Wacholz
Art Director: Bob Lentz

Cataloging-in-Publication Data is available
at the Library of Congress website.

ISBN: 978-1-62370-953-2

Printed and bound in the USA.
010848S18